Goodnight, Daniel Tiger

written by Angela C. Santomero

To Hope and Ella.
Everything I do, I do for you!
I'm so proud of you both, and
honored to be your mom!
Ugga Mugga, Mommy

Simon Spotlight

New York London Toronto Sydney New Delhi

It was a beautiful day in the neighborhood today, and now it is nighttime. Daniel Tiger needs to get ready for bed! "Ding, ding, ding!" says Daniel, "Tigey wants to go for a trolley ride!"

Daniel wants to play, but . . . it's time to get ready for bed.

"I know you want to play," Mom says as she snuggles with Daniel, "but sleep is important so that you can grow. Do you remember what we do to get ready for bed?"

Daniel smiles and sings with Mom, *"Bathtime, pj's, brush teeth, story and song, and off to bed!"*

"Ding, ding! Hop aboard for a trolley ride to bathtime!"
Dad says.
Daniel laughs and takes a ride. "Ding, ding!"
Daniel wants to play, but . . . it's time to get ready for bed.

Daniel likes bathtime! As he scrubs, he plays and sings, "*Scrub, scrub, scrub my fur, up on top my head! Scrubby-scrubby-scrubby-scrub, soon it's time for bed!*"

Daniel imagines he is on a boat sailing the soapy seas. He sings, "Sailing, sailing, sailing the soapy seas. Bring all your friends and come with me to sail the soapy seas!"

Daniel wants to play, but . . . it's time to get ready for bed.
Dad says, "You need to go to sleep at bedtime so that your
great big imagination can rest."
"I do have a lot of imagining I want to do
tomorrow!" Daniel says as Dad dries his fur.

Daniel sings, *"Bathtime, pj's, brush teeth, story and song, and off to bed!"* Daniel has taken his bath and now it's time for his favorite trolley pj's.

"Next stop on the trolley ride is brush your teeth," says Dad. Daniel takes his toothbrush and hops up to the sink.

Daniel sings, "I gotta brusha, brusha, brush, brush my teeth at night if I want to keep them healthy and bright. I gotta brusha, brusha, brusha, brush my teeth!" Daniel's teeth are all brushed!

"Let's take Tigey for a ride on Trolley," says Daniel.
"Ding, ding, ding!"
Daniel wants to play, but . . . it's time to get ready for bed.

Mom holds Tigey up to her ear, "Oh, I see," she says to Tigey. Daniel stops playing and looks at Mom. What is she talking about with Tigey?

"Tigey wants to snuggle up in bed and hear a bedtime story," Mom explains.

Daniel climbs up into bed. "Let's read a bedtime story . . . for Tigey," he says. Daniel is getting sleepy.

Daniel snuggles up with Mom as she reads a bedtime story. Reading a story with Mom makes Daniel feel comfy and cozy. Daniel is sleepy. Daniel *does* want to go to bed.

Daniel quietly sings, *"Bathtime, pj's, brush teeth, story and song, and off to bed."* Then he yawns a big tired tiger yawn. Daniel does want to go to bed. Daniel is sleepy.

"Mom and Dad, can you sing me my goodnight song?"

Mom and Dad sing, "Goodnight, Daniel, goodnight. It's time to go to sleep and when you awake, the sun will greet you with its bright and sunny face. Goodnight, Daniel, goodnight." Everyone in the neighborhood is going to sleep too.

Goodnight, Miss Elaina, goodnight.

Goodnight, Prince Wednesday, goodnight.

Goodnight, Katerina Kittycat, goodnight.

Goodnight, Daniel Tiger, goodnight. And goodnight to YOU.
Ugga Mugga!